Naila Suraiya is a proud Bangladeshi-American living in Texas since 1995. She is a lifelong advocate for children's education and has worked with young people from pre-school to high school ages. Her favorite experiences working in various public and private schools involved the sharing of stories in any form. Naila believes stories bring connection and encourage a deeper understanding of each other's similarities and an appreciation of each other's differences. She is passionate about raising sensitivity and awareness toward immigrants in our communities because although we may look and sound different, we can enrich our relationships through our different stories and find common ground for beautiful friendships.

Copyright © Naila Suraiya 2022

All rights reserved. No part of this publication may be reproduced, distributed, or transmitted in any form or by any means, including photocopying, recording, or other electronic or mechanical methods, without the prior written permission of the publisher, except in the case of brief quotations embodied in critical reviews and certain other non-commercial uses permitted by copyright law. For permission requests, write to the publisher.

Any person who commits any unauthorized act in relation to this publication may be liable to criminal prosecution and civil claims for damages.

Ordering Information
Quantity sales: Special discounts are available on quantity purchases by corporations, associations, and others. For details, contact the publisher at the address below.

Publisher's Cataloging-in-Publication data
Suraiya, Naila
Just Like Us

ISBN 9781638292906 (Paperback)
ISBN 9781638292913 (Hardback)
ISBN 9781638292920 (ePub e-book)

Library of Congress Control Number: 2022904706

www.austinmacauley.com/us

First Published 2022
Austin Macauley Publishers LLC
40 Wall Street, 33rd Floor, Suite 3302
New York, NY 10005
USA

mail-usa@austinmacauley.com
+1 (646) 5125767

To all the children of the Muslim immigrants who strive to prove that they are just like everybody else.

I am grateful to my husband, Anis, who has always provided steadfast support to all my creative projects; to my daughter, Samreen, for going over the first draft with an eagle eye, and to my daughter, Baursha, for her eloquent feedback on the first illustrations. This book would not have come to life without the vivid illustrations produced by the gifted artist, Caroline Webb, who not only has incredible talent, but also a keen insight to feel the rhythms of the author's heartbeat. Finally, I am immensely indebted to my publisher, Austin Macauley, for placing their trust in a first-time author like me and helping to make my dream come true.

Jenny stood in her lawn.

The last items were loaded in the U-haul in the driveway next to their house.
Her best friend, Ashley, and her family were moving out today.
Ashley had been her best friend for as many years as she had lived in her neighborhood.

Finally, everything was loaded and ready to go. Ashley walked up slowly across the lawn and stood at the edge of Jenny's driveway, clutching her favorite teddy bear. Their eyes met for a minute before tears welled up.

"Bye," was all Ashley could manage to whisper, before she turned her back and hurried back to join her parents in their van, almost scared to look back. Jenny's mouth quivered silently, as she raised a limp hand to wave goodbye. She stood in her driveway, never taking her eyes off Ashley as their van rolled out in a cloud of dust.

The next day, Jenny watched the 'For Sale' sign go up in the middle of the lawn next door.

Every now and then, Jenny would eagerly look out the living room windows to find new families dropping in, but the house remained empty for a long time.

Then, one sunny weekend, a truck pulled into Ashley's driveway. Peering out the window, Jenny felt her heart beating really, really fast. The 'For Sale' sign was being removed.

The next day, a Uhaul pulled into the driveway next door. A van pulled in right behind it.

Jenny leaned forward to catch a good glimpse of the new family.

But what she saw came as a bizarre surprise. First, out of the Uhaul stepped out the Dad. His face was covered with a thick black beard that reminded her of a pirate. He was not in jeans or a T-shirt, but a flowing tunic that reached down to his knees, underneath which his baggy trousers flapped in the breeze.

As Jenny wondered why he was dressed like that, out stepped the Mom from the van.

She was dressed in a flowing long-sleeved robe that reached down to her ankles. Even her head was tightly wrapped in layers of soft material like a turban, revealing only her face. Jenny was vaguely reminded of the evil Queen Maleficent from Snow White and the Seven Dwarfs. She had never seen any of her friends' moms or dads dressed like that before.

As Jenny stared wide-eyed at her weird new neighbors, her eyes fell upon another little person climbing out of the back seat. Out stepped a little girl with dark hair and hazel eyes, clutching a stuffed doll. Jenny's heart leapt with joy! Finally, someone to play with! And she was wearing a Pink T-shirt with jeans and seemed to be Jenny's age too. Yay!

For the next few days, Jenny was peering out her living room window three times a day, hoping to see the new girl come out into the front lawn; but all she could see were more cars pulling up and more moms and dads going into Ashley's house that now belonged to the new family.

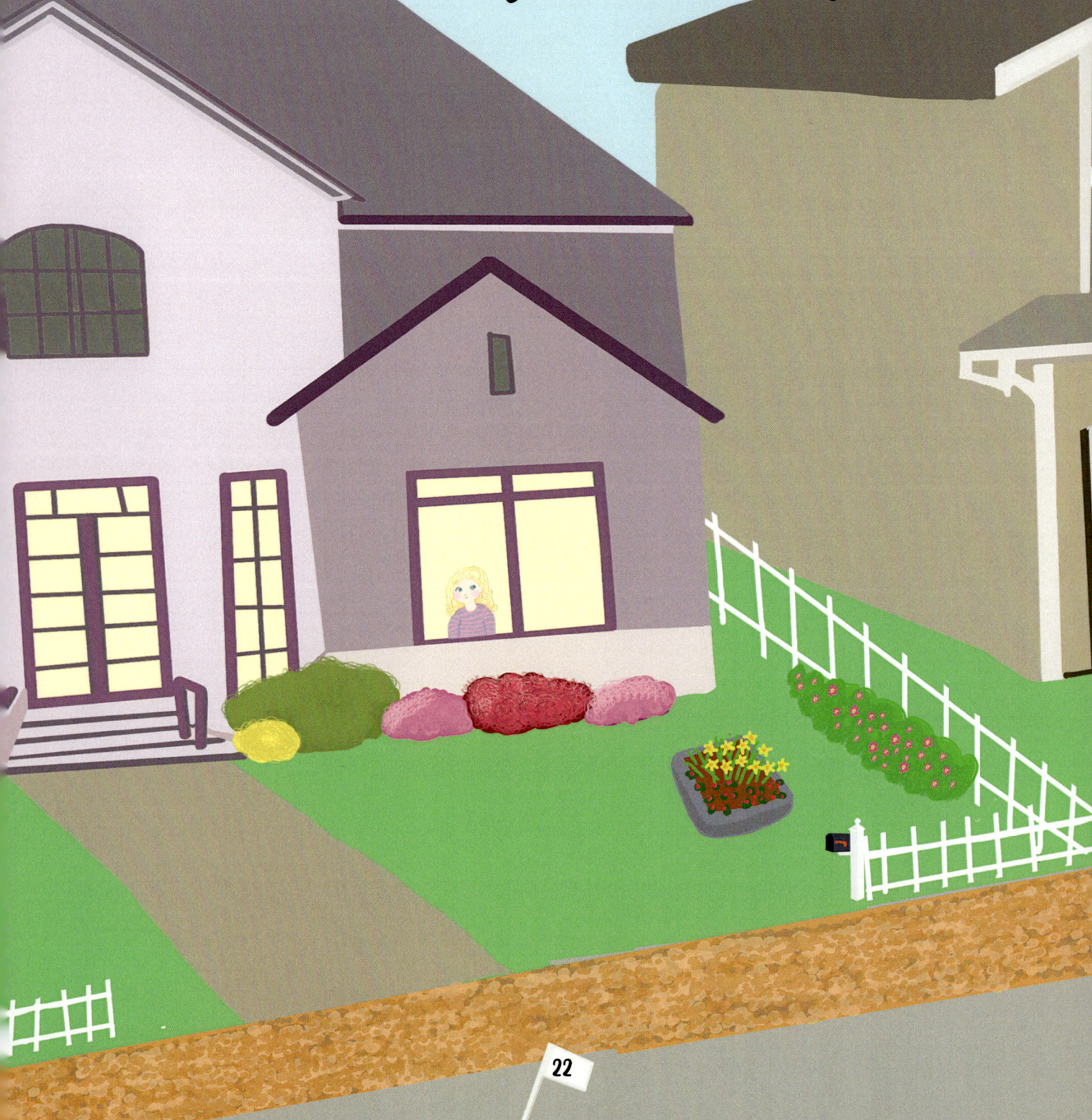

And these moms were clad in the same dark flowy robes; the dads wore the same thick beards, the same loose tunics and baggy pants.

Sometimes Jenny would wake up around a little past three in the morning and push back the curtains on her bedroom window to see a light on in a bedroom next door. She tried to listen in for voices, but all was quiet. The light stayed on for an hour or so before going out.

What could people possibly be doing at these wee hours of the morning? Jenny had read enough mystery novels to know that this was the best time to hold all secret meetings. She felt her blood curdling with fear.

A few weeks after her new neighbors had moved in, it was time to celebrate the Fourth of July. This was one of Jenny's favorite holidays of the summer not only because of the fireworks, but also because of the backyard bar-be-que that she so eagerly looked forward to.

Jenny fondly remembered how they would have Ashley's family over and spend the day grilling and playing games in their backyard.

But this time it was different. Biting on the perfectly charbroiled ribs dad had scooped into her plate, Jenny couldn't help glancing over the fence every now and then, hoping to see her new neighbors come out into the backyard.

She knew they were at home. Their big van was parked right outside. But not a soul came outside the entire day.

Then one Saturday, Jenny overheard the mom and the dad talking in their driveway. She knew it was none of her business, but Jenny couldn't help leaning against her fence to eavesdrop on their conversation.

But she couldn't understand a word of it! The sounds came out of their mouths with bizarre thrusts. Surely that had to be their Martian language!

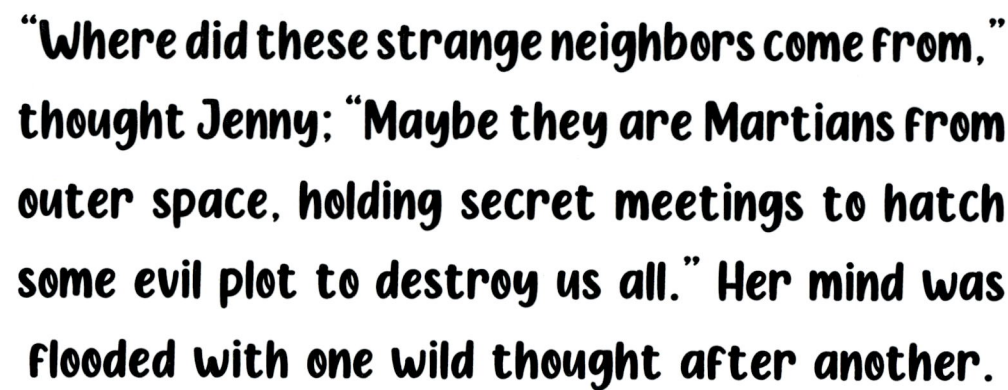

"Where did these strange neighbors come from," thought Jenny; "Maybe they are Martians from outer space, holding secret meetings to hatch some evil plot to destroy us all." Her mind was flooded with one wild thought after another.

One night at the dinner table, Jenny couldn't hold it in any longer. As Mom scooped some salad onto her plate, Jenny blurted out: "Mom... Our new neighbors... are they from another planet? They look so strange!"
"Don't be silly, dear," Mom smiled back. "They are people, just like us. They just dress differently. They are from a far-away land."

But Jenny wasn't reassured. She finished her dinner quietly.

The next day dawned bright and sunny. Jenny sat on the swing in her backyard, thinking of what Ashley might be doing right now in her new town.

All of a sudden, her eyes fell on a little figure in Ashley's backyard. It was the new girl. She slowly walked out of their back door and stood under the huge pecan tree in the corner. Jenny thought she looked like the saddest girl on the planet.

Then she looked up. Their eyes met. For the first few seconds, it felt really awkward. Then Jenny managed to get the words out of her mouth, "Hi! Do you wanna come play?"

The hazel eyes lit up. She nodded her head, smiling.

"Ask your Mom first. Then come in from the side," yelled Jenny, pointing toward the direction of the side-door in their fence.

Hanaan was from Syria. They had moved to the US when she was three. As the two chatted away, Jenny found that like her, Hannan's favorite color was pink and she also loved pizza. They both loved to read. The time seemed to fly by so fast!

"Hanaan, It's time for lunch," a sing-song voice finally stopped them in their tracks. Both girls looked up to see Hanaan's mom at their backdoor.

She didn't have the dark robe or layered turban on today and was wearing a really colorful outfit with long sleeves that came down below her knees, paired with ankle-length baggy pants. She had the same hazel eyes as Hanaan and the most beautiful face.
"Why don't you come and join us?"
she looked up at Jenny with a smile.

Jenny ran in to get her Mom's permission before she rushed into Hanaan's house. The whole house was filled with the aroma of freshly baked pizza. "Homemade pizza. Wow!" It was the best pizza Jenny had ever tasted.

That night at the dinner table, Jenny was the happiest little eight-year-old as she told her mom, "Mom, you know what? You were right about our new neighbors; they are just like us."

Mom looked down at Jenny's beaming face:
"I know, honey; they are people...
Just like us."